GOOD NIGHT, SLEEP TIGHT

Written by
MEM FOX

Illustrated by
JUDY HORACEK

Orchard Books • An Imprint of Scholastic Inc. • New York

For Michael Williams — M.F.

For Oscar — J.H.

E
Fox,
Mem

Good Night, Sleep Tight was originally published in Australia by
Scholastic Australia Pty Limited in 2012.
This U.S. edition was published under license from Scholastic Australia Pty Limited.

Library of Congress Cataloging-in-Publication Data Available

ISBN 978-0-545-53370-6 (HC)   ISBN 978-0-545-55463-3 (PB)

10 9 8 7 6 5 4 3 2 1   13 14 15 16 17

Printed in Malaysia   46
First U.S. printing, August 2013

The display type was hand-lettered and set in Baby Doll.
The text was set in Bopee and laCartoonerie.

One Friday night, Bonnie and Ben were being looked after by their favorite babysitter.

Skinny Doug leaned against

their bedroom door and said:

"Good night, sleep tight.
Hope the fleas don't bite!
If they do,
squeeze 'em tight
and they won't bite
another night!"

"We love it! We love it!" said Bonnie and Ben.

"How does it go? Will you say it again?"

"Some other time," said Skinny Doug.

"But I'll tell you another
I heard from my mother:

It's raining! It's pouring!

The old man is snoring.

He went to bed
and bumped his head

and couldn't get up in the morning."

"We love it! We love it!" said Bonnie and Ben.

"How does it go? Will you say it again?"

"Some other time," said Skinny Doug.

"But I'll tell you another
I heard from my mother:

This little piggy
went to market.
This little piggy
stayed home.

This little piggy
had roast beef,
and this little piggy
had none.

"We love it! We love it!" said Bonnie and Ben.

"How does it go? Will you say it again?"

"Some other time," said Skinny Doug.

"But I'll tell you another

I heard from my mother:

Pat-a-cake, pat-a-cake, baker's man,

bake me a cake as fast as you can.

Roll it and pat it and mark it with 'B'

and put it in the oven for baby and me!"

"We love it! We love it!" said Bonnie and Ben.

"How does it go? Will you say it again?"

"Some other time," said Skinny Doug.

"But I'll tell you another

I heard from my mother:

one step,

two steps,

and tickle under there!"

"We love it! We love it!" said Bonnie and Ben.

"How does it go? Will you say it again?"

"Some other time," said Skinny Doug.

"But I'll tell you another
I heard from my mother:

This is the way
the ladies ride:
trit, trot,
trit, trot.

This is the way
the gentlemen ride:
clip, clop,
clip, clop.

And this is the way the farmers ride:
bumpety, bumpety,
bumpety, bumpety,
bumpety,
bumpety, BUMP!"

TRIT TROT TRIT TROT

CLIP CLOP CLIP CLOP TRIT TROT

BUMPETY BUMPETY

"We love it! We love it!" said Bonnie and Ben.

"How does it go? Will you say it again?"

"Some other time," said Skinny Doug.

"But I'll tell you another

I heard from my mother:

Star light, star bright, first star I see tonight.

I wish I may, I wish I might

have the wish I wish tonight."

"We love it! We love it!" said Bonnie and Ben.

"How does it go? Will you say it again?"

"Look, you two," said Skinny Doug,

"it's long past your bedtime.

It's time for sleep now, okay? So . . .

GOOD

NIGHT,

SLEEP TIGHT!"